Moses Owen

Plymouth Church and Other Poems

Moses Owen

Plymouth Church and Other Poems

ISBN/EAN: 9783744722582

Printed in Europe, USA, Canada, Australia, Japan

Cover: Foto ©Andreas Hilbeck / pixelio.de

More available books at **www.hansebooks.com**

PLYMOUTH CHURCH,

AND

OTHER POEMS.

MOSES OWEN.

PORTLAND:

PUBLISHED BY W. S. JONES.

1873.

HARMON & JERRIS,

PRINTERS,

PORTLAND, ME.

PREFACE.

Having been solicited by many of my friends to collect my fugitive pieces, and give them a local habitation and a name, I have done so, and trust an indulgent public will receive this little volume with the same favor that it did my previous one.

PLYMOUTH CHURCH,

AND

OTHER POEMS.

CONTENTS.

PLYMOUTH CHURCH.

OW much's the bid for this
    broad-aisle pew?
Four hundred dollars! — 'twill
    never do!
Five hundred — six — did I just
    hear eight?
The road to heaven from thence is straight."

Ah, an old *Saint* nods! he has gained the prize,
And he pays with tears wrung from widows'
    eyes;

Yet the Auctioneer, with a smile and nod,
Keeps on: "How much do I hear for God!"

The broad-aisle God is a different thing
From the God for sale in an obscure wing;
Yet I often wonder if He is more'
At Plymouth front than at Plymouth door!

Is He there at all with the pampered throng?
Does He like the music and well-paid song?
Do the rustling silks and studied prayer,
Keep Him from common worship *there?*

And I often muse to myself, alone,
If seats are sold 'round the heavenly throne!
Ah, yes, my friend! they are sold above,
But the price is paid on this earth in love!

And earth's down-trodden need have no fear,
For Christ has risen — He has been here!
From the cruel cross, with spear pierced through,
He went not up from a broad-aisle pew!

To the dying thief, with his death-glazed eyes,

He said: "This day . . . . . in Paradise!"
And the heavens grew dark as earth did moan,
And thunders muttered — "the Cross, the
    Throne!"

*   *   *   *   *   *   *   *   *   *   *   *   *

"How much, how much, for another seat!
It's going, gone! — Ah, Religion's sweet!"
Yet, Auctioneer, 'tis a fearful thought
That a God of Justice cannot be bought!

THE "CITY OF BOSTON."

The following verses were written at a time when although the greatest anxiety was felt for the safety of this noble vessel, yet hopes were entertained that she might come safely into port. But, alas! days have lengthened into weeks, weeks into months, months into years, and Despair gazes sadly out on the wild waste of waters that gives no answer. The sea keepeth well its secret, and it can only be known that she sailed from port and came not back.

THERE comes no voice to-night
from that drear waste,
Where rolls Atlantic 'neath the
dark'ning sky,
Whose foam-crowned billows
with impetuous haste,
Scorn all control, nor pause to give reply.

I hear the cruel gale, fresh from the deep,
Now, landward, howl its prowess to the
night;

In vain Love asks it where her treasures sleep —
   It gives no token — speaks but of its might!

I picture to myself a storm-tossed bark,
   'Neath icy mountains battling with despair;
The final crash — the blank — then all grows
   dark,
   And heaven alone records the shriek or
   prayer.

And still the seas chase on as though in play,
   And still the ice-bergs thund'ring rise and
   fall,
And naught save man's poor work has passed
   away —
   None knoweth why, save One who knoweth
   all.

'Twere vain to ask the tomb how sleep its dead,
   'Twere vain to ask the wave what lies
   beneath;
Yet tomb and wave combined need have no
   dread,

For Hope o'er each points to the victor's
wreath.

The sun may rise and set, yet tell no tale,
  The seasons come and go, yet whisper not,
And quivering lips, alone, all deathly pale,
  May murmur: "Gone — unheard of — not
  forgot!"

God grant she rides the waves and yet may
  come
  Safe from the ocean with her precious freight;
Stout hearts are beating, and though lips be
  dumb,
Yet Love proclaims that she can longer wait.

God grant the best! our hopes, our prayers,
  our fears,
  Are out to-night upon the ocean's foam;
May ne'er Despair proclaim with bitter tears,
  She sailed triumphant but she came not home.

PITY ME;

OR,

THE CHILD'S LAMENT.

———

PITY me, pity me, earth seems so
 drear,
Dark are the shadows that fall o'er
 life's path;
Naught that is beautiful smiles on
 me here,
Pity a child that has known only wrath!
Out in the graveyard my mother lies sleeping,
Softly the summer rains over her weeping;
Heart-broken died she in life's early morn,
Earth grew so dark when my mother was gone.

Heart-broken died she, the Summer winds
    sighing,
Tell of a father, a loved one defiled;
Pity him, Heaven, for mother when dying,
Blessed him and wept for her husband
    and child.

Bright dreams of morning you smile not on
    me —
Only a drunkard's child ! That is my name.
Father in heaven thy child turns to thee,
    Thou knowest the heart, thou art ever the
    same.
Poor earthly father the foul fiends possessing,
Father on high, Oh, grant him thy blessing !
    Mother is pleading, a poor child doth moan,
    Bless him, O Father, and smile from thy
    throne !

Often at evening some bright shining star
    Looks down upon me and twinkles its love;
Mother's in heaven, and heaven's not far,

5

And earth's down-trodden shall triumph
  above.
Who bears the cross in fell anguish and sorrow,
May wear the crown on a bright sunny morrow;
  Mother in heaven, Oh, list to my prayer!
  Teach me, thy child, how that cross I shall
    bear.

THE ORPHANS' HOME AT BATH.

VERSES WRITTEN FOR THE CHILDREN.

ES, the prayers our fathers
 whispered when they left this
 mortal shore,
That their darlings be protected,
 uttered 'midst the battle's roar,
Have been answered, and God's
angels brought good tidings from above,
And the "Home" uprose in glory, crowned
with brightness, and with love.

Blessed angels! blessed tidings!
 Weary feet no more must roam;
Love has crowned our earthly dwelling,
 Love shall crown our heavenly home.

Striving e'er to reach perfection, let us one
    another cheer,
We are brothers, sisters, loved ones — heaven's
    not far, 'tis almost here!
Let our prayers by night and morning rise from
    loving hearts above,
Blessed angels, blessed fathers, who have
    crowned the work with love!

    Blessed angels! Blessed tidings!
      Weary feet no more must roam;
    Love has crowned our earthly dwelling,
      Love shall crown our heavenly home.

TO HENRY TUCKER,

AUTHOR OF "STAR OF THE EVENING," "WHEN THIS CRUEL WAR IS OVER," &c.

H thou, whose ballads touch the
heart,
Sweet flowing as the lark's
clear song,
Whose every tone doth joy impart,
To thee our love and praise belong.

When "cruel war" swept o'er the land,
Thy gentle strains e'en then could cheer,
Those chords struck by a master-hand,
Still echo in the sigh and tear.

'Twas thine to move with magic power,
　　And waken thoughts long deemed as dead,
And all entranced in fairy bower,
　　The blissful laden moments fled.

The maid at eve has turned her eyes
　　Up to the star-lit skies above her,
And thy sweet song has checked her sighs,
　　And brought her near an absent lover.

The soldier on th' ensanguined field,
　　Amidst the wounded and the slain,
Beneath the moon in awe has kneeled,
　　And prayed that they might meet again.

· Sweet Singer, let the wreath be placed,
　　E'er to keep green, upon thy brow,
And of the many it has graced,
　　None are more worthy than art thou.

POEM

DELIVERED AT BATH ON THE SECOND ANNIVERSARY OF
DECORATING THE GRAVES OF THE SOLDIERS WITH FLOWERS,
JUNE 10, 1869.

ONE year ago, and 'neath a
cloudless sky,
Our hearts beat fast and kindled
every eye;
Beneath you shaft we stood and
all around
Bespoke the solemn scene — 'twas hallowed
ground.
Not far away, where, with slow-measured tread,
The long ranks passed the city of the dead,
There loving hearts and hands bestrewed
with flowers
Each lowly mound, — the time, the day was
ours.

The mother brought her wreath; her boy went
   forth,
She knew his valor and his modest worth;
   The night was long, replete with sigh and
      groan,
   The morning came at last — his name is on
      the stone!
She did not weep, but, silent, drained the cup,
He was his country's, and she gave him up;
   And Freedom's temple with such names shall
      glow,
   The Soldier's from above — the Mother's
      from below.

One year ago! Since then the snows have shed
Their white-robed mantle o'er our hallowed
   dead;
   The bleak North winds have mourned their
      requiems chill,
   And sobbed their dirges to this barren hill;
But yet we know that Nature soon would
   spring
To blooming life, that summer birds would sing

That fragrant flowers would scent the evening
    breeze,
And music whisper from the rustling trees.
    The seasons change but love knows not a
      blight,
    Nor winter's frost can harm, nor day nor
      night,
It grows the stronger through the length'ning
    years —
Oh, hallowed Dead! 'tis love we give, not tears.
    You need .no tears, your winter has been
      passed,
Eternal summer meets your view at last.
Your furlough came and never more to roam,
Your Captain took you to his own loved home.

We call you dead! This day we set apart
To write each name upon a Nation's heart;
    For all we have and are we owe to thee —
    A country saved, our homes, our liberty!
Up to the skies I look! Immortal ranks
Accept a Nation's prayers, a Nation's thanks!
  6

. Our words are weak and silence speaketh best:
  Speak on, O Stone, the glory of the blessed !

They are not dead.! They ever hover near
To check the sigh, to dry the falling tear;
  Tell me ye Winds that round yon shaft do play,
  Are they not present in our midst to-day ?
Immortal day ! thy every moment fraught
With memory's tear and memory's pleasing
    thought :
  'Tis sweet to know that love surmounts the
    tomb
  And lives transplanted from this earthly
    gloom ;
It knows no death, for death with it is life,
It carries us beyond this mortal strife,
  'Tis God's best gift to earth, 'tis heaven's
    pure ray,
  And neath its brightness do we stand this day.
As long as yonder stream shall have its flow,
Or you bright sun shall give the morning's glow,

As long as days and nights and seasons roll,
This earth shall cherish each immortal soul.

Flowers for the dead!—This sweet memorial
    day
Should waft its fragrance and our griefs allay,
    Should draw us nearer to the loved and
    blessed,
And be a day of peace, a day of rest.
Sweet Peace has come and smiling o'er the land
Has scattered blessings with no sparing hand,
    Dispelled the gloom and bade war's thun-
    ders cease —
    Let us remember those who brought that
    peace!

The Dead and Living! Marching side by side
You scarce were conscious when your comrades
    died;
    The roll was called when closed the hard-
    fought day,
    But lips replied not that had closed for aye.

They gave their all and only prayed that those,
Their children dear, be sheltered from earth's
 woes;
Our Soldier's Orphan's!—shall they not be
 dear?
A Sampson spoke—that prayer was answered
 here!

Around that Home affection's flowers shall
 spring,
And cheerful voices shall loud anthems sing;
Ope wide the doors and let the words be said:
Love for the living and our martyred dead!

The day we cherish! let it ever stand
A Day of Memory to a ransomed land!

MOTHER.

MAY 25, 1869.

OT in her dear loved home our
    Mother moves to-day,
God sent his angels down to
    bear his saint away;
She uttered no 'complaint, She
    knew her God was kind,
She only mourned for those, her children,
    left behind.

Our eyes were dimmed with tears, we could
    not see that throng,
Nor hear one note that rose from that triumph-
    ant song!

Up from the feeble clay an immortal soul had
   risen,
And but a smile remained around its earthly
   prison.

Oh, saintly form that sleeps in yonder church-
   yard drear,
Thy child yet hears thy voice which tells him
   thou art near;
The love thou gav'st on earth, shines brighter
   from above—
Thy children weeping here, need all a mother's
   love.

HAUNTED.

THERE is a house in Bath, a
dread abode,
Haunted by goblins through
the livelong night;
Belated travelers shun its passing road,
And only mention in their tones of fright.

Long since deserted, unto swift decay
It passes surely and must soon be gone;
Yet every night each window shows a ray,
And lights keep dancing through its rooms
till morn.

And hideous sounds are heard, appalling moans,

As demon answers demon with a shriek,
And fearful struggles blend with frightful
  groans,
  Sounding more awful than the tongue can
  speak.

The bat flies o'er it on his way at night,
  Nor stays a guest within its darkened room;
Darkness but claims it and the shades of fright,
  And spectral forms but haunt its solemn
  gloom.

Some tell of murder done long since therein,
  Blood-curdling stories of a wretch's hate;
And o'er that house must rest the blight of sin,
  Nor Hope dare enter through its cursed gate.

Be it as it may be, we only know
  There is a house in Bath where goblins dwell;
The wearied traveler sees its windows glow,
  And knows 'tis peopled by the hosts of hell.

* * * * * * * * * * * * *

There is a house in Bath — ah, more than one,
　Not yet deserted, where bad spirits stay;
Where love should dwell, by passion 'tis undone,
　Where hate and anger hold divided sway;

Where brother answers brother in the strife,
　Where curse but follows curse the whole day
　　through,
Where bitter feelings are forever rife,
　Where souls are haunted by a goblin crew.

THE

RETURNED MAINE BATTLE FLAGS.

———

OTHING but flags — but simple
   flags,
   Tattered and torn and hanging in
   rags ;
   And we walk beneath them with
   careless tread,
Nor think of the hosts of the mighty dead,
That have marched beneath them in days gone
      by,
With a burning cheek and a kindling eye,
And have bathed their folds with their young
      life's tide,

And, dying, blessed them, and, blessing, died.

Nothing but flags — yet, methinks, at night
They tell each other their tales of fright;
And dim spectres come and their thin arms
    twine
'Round each standard torn as they stand in line!
As the word is given — they charge! they form!
And the dim hall rings with the battle's storm!
And once again through the smoke and strife,
Those colors lead to a Nation's life.

Nothing but flags — yet they're bathed with
    tears,
They tell of triumphs, of hopes, of fears;
Of a mother's prayers, of a boy away,
Of a serpent crushed, of the coming day!
Silent, they speak, and the tear will start
As we stand beneath them with throbbing heart,
And think of those who are ne'er forgot,
Their flags come home — why come *they* not?

Nothing but flags — yet we hold our breath,

And gaze with awe at those types of death!
Nothing but flags, yet the thought will come,
The heart must pray though the lips be dumb!
They are sacred, pure, and we see no stain
On those dear loved flags at home again ;
Baptized in blood, our purest, best,
Tattered and torn they're now at rest.

THE

THE
MAINE GENERAL HOSPITAL FAIR.

 STATE, united, hastes with loving
    hands,
    To wreathe sweet garlands that can
      never fade;
    Love binds each flower with her soft
      silken bands,
Her voice is gentle, yet it is obeyed.
Proud as an emblem of protecting care,
  The walls uprise to shield each suffering one;
And high o'er all floats sweetly on the air,
  Oh, Sunrise State, thy crown is nobly won!
Sweet time of June! thy length'ning days shall
    bring

Treasures untold to crown the Summer's day;
Each blade of grass and fragrant flower shall
    sing,
    That Love keeps watch and ward for aye
    and aye.
The farthest east speaks to the distant west,
    And north and south clasp hands at Mercy's
    call;
The feast is ready — no reluctant guest
    Comes to the table Love has spread for all.
What nobler thought than in the human heart
    Sweet Pity finds a place nor yet has flown;
Does Sorrow call? — the tear unchecked will
    start,
    And Love proclaims that Maine will guard
    her own.

THE

SOLDIERS' MONUMENT.

IS but a shaft on the windy
    height,
Which will crumble to dust by
    the ages' blight,
And the names will fade from
    the stone away,
In the long, long years — yet they count to-day!

'Tis but a shaft — yet we bow the head,
And feel we are nearer our noble dead ;
We watched them going with tear-dimmed eye,
And clasping hand, and fond "good-bye !"
And the rolling drums, and the flags unfurled,
Told not of the shock that should shake the
    world,

Of those fearful years, when, in battle's strife,
They should give their own for a Nation's life.

We saw not the spectres that followed on,
Yet, somehow, we wept when we found them
    gone;
And many a heart felt itself alone,
Though it read no name on the unwrought
    stone.

'Tis but a shaft — and our valiant dead
Perchance sleep far from its rocky bed;
Yet I love to think that they hover 'round,
At home once more near this hallowed ground,
And all unseen, with their words of cheer,
They whisper: " Mother, your boy is near! "
And I love to think that their toils are o'er,
They form no ranks — hear no cannon's roar !
They have passed beyond — all their work is
    done.
They have fought the fight and the victory's
    won.

Oh, valiant Dead! though that shaft decay,
And crumble and sink into dust away,
Yet nobler than cunning works of art,
Your temple stands in Freedom's heart!
And brighter and brighter your names shall
    glow,
For they shine on high though they fade below,
And eternal years may not blight nor chill,
Though that shaft must sink from the windy
    hill.

AN ACROSTIC.

MAY heaven protect our dear
        loved State,
And may she stand supremely
        great!
In noble deeds let her delight,
Nor strive but in the cause of
Right!
Each cry for succor may she hear,
Grant that she bend the listening ear!
E'er let her children claim her care,
Nor Sorrow speak to empty air!
Enduring though the Nations fall,
Raising the weak and blessing all,

As first she greets the morning sun,
Let love keep bright till time be run!
Honor and fame shall wreathe her brow,
On every hill glad Heralds now
Sing songs of praise and every plain
Prolongs the rapturous song o'er Maine.
In sunlight first "Dirigo" gleams,
The mountains whisper to her streams,
And over all in might and sway,
Love tells her story all the day.

ON GUARD.

IS night — and the Sentinel
      paces his round,
   With an eye for each object, an
      ear for each sound ;
   But his thoughts are roving long,
      long miles away,
They speed from him swiftly like children to
   play.

Again he's at home in a fond wife's embrace,
And tear chases tear down his sun-beaten face ;
His children now greet him, now call him by
   name,
He heeds not the night-watch — his home is the
   same.

Still green is the vine that encircles the door,
The path is the same as in blest days of yore;
Aye, every loved object stands clear to his view,
God's angels have blessed him — inspired him
    anew!

"Oh, bless'd be home!" now springs from his
    heart;
And blest be the ties that earth's powers cannot
    part,
And blessed be memory that spark from God's
    throne,
That star for earth's mariner wandering alone.

And blessed be our country — our Flag of the
    Free,
That floats now in triumph o'er land and o'er
    sea,
And proud in thy glory we see thee arise,
As the sun scatters clouds in his course through
    the skies.

The Sentinel's pacing his dull, dreary round,
His soul is now free though the body be
   bound, —
But hark! through the darkness some sound
   strikes his ear,
He stops as some object doth dimly appear.

"Halt!" cries he; "Who comes!" speaks the
   Sentinel now;
"A friend with the countersign!" 's answered
   him low;
"Advance with the countersign!" Soon it is
   given,
His home is now earth whilst before it was
   heaven.

That bright dream is over! his home's far
   away,
The night breeze is speaking that round him
   doth play,
It tells of a country that's dearer than life,
And his arm feels the stronger for Freedom's
   own strife.

It tells of a foe who would pluck the bright
stars
From a flag so triumphant in peace or in wars;
Who would make it a by-word — an object of
shame,
And he says: "I will die for its freedom and
fame!"

And blessed is a country with stout hearts like
these,
The tramp of her armies is swelling the breeze,
They rush to her rescue, their lives freely give,
'Twere better to die than in bondage to live.

God bless thee, O Sentinel, pacing thy round,
Safe may'st thou return with the Victor's
wreath bound,
When the dark clouds of war shall have passed
from the skies,
And rebellion is hurled down — never to rise!

JEALOUSY.

O H, thou disturber of the immortal mind,
Where shall we find a demon of
thy kind?
E'en trifles light as air, 'neath
thy control,
Become as mountains to the doubting soul.

Thou sparest nothing in thy withering blight,
Thou turnest joy to pain — our days to night;
Thou rendest ties that God made from above,
And 'neath thy influence what is left of love?

Nor reason claims thee, it is all unknown,

But passion, lust and rapine are thine own ;
And 'neath thy baleful pall comes fell despair,
Nor peace can rest if Jealousy be there.

Give me a lowly cot — a happy mind —
One that I love, and far from human kind,
In sweet contentment I could pass my days,
And songs of joy in grateful homage raise.

TO WHOM?

OMEWHERE I knew, at some
good time,
In no far place nor distant clime,
I should meet one whom dreams
alone,
Had dared to let me call my own.

The sailor on the stormy sea,
Ne'er looked for light more wistfully,
Than I for one who should be true,
I found it nameless one in you!

O happy Eve! the star of love
Looked down and smiled from heaven above,

My wandering steps were turned aside,
And that bright star I then espied.

The time we met shall ever be
A sacred day of Memory;
For some kind angel led me where
I looked and found you standing there.

And thus we met and though time flies,
Yet love still kindles in your eyes,
And that bright eve can ne'er seem far
When heaven first showed a guiding star.

AT LAST.

———◦✦◦———

AT last my short-lived Joys have sunk
    in sorrow,
  And night and darkness have
    usurped their reign ;
'Twas but a day that brought such
    gloomy morrow,
For one has gone who may not come again.

At last the pitcher carried often has been
    broken,
  The silver chord is loosed — all hope is fled,
Yet still I linger though the word be spoken
  That bids me wander from the saintly dead.

At last! I knew that all earth's joys were
    fleeting,
  Yet still I fondly hoped 'twas not my fate,
And life sped on with glad and merry greeting—
  A day so golden could not longer wait.

My thoughts go back to that glad sunny
    morning,
When life was young and earth and sky seemed
    bright,
Oh happy day, that brought such glorious
    dawning
How could you leave me in such gloomy night!

In vain, in vain, I ask! the breeze is sighing,
  The crimson leaves now flutter from the trees,
And Nature speaks e'en in her very dying:
  Go seek your answer — it is found in these!

TO THE KENNEBEC.

OH,   sweet flowing River, how
        oft by thy side,
    In childhood's loved days I
        have wandered along,
    When the world was all bright
        and my thoughts like thy tide,
Danced out to an ocean of music and song.

Thou still art the same — but, alas, I am not!
Grown older, the charm and the freshness
    have fled ;

Some friends that I loved have grown cold,
   have forgot —
   And some now are sleeping the sleep of the
   dead.

Your white-winged ships you still bear to the
   sea,
   I *once* thought that pleasure must follow
   them on;
And far o'er the waters my thoughts went with
   thee,
   They went into dream-land, where I too was
   gone.

I know *now* that tempest and darkness and
   gloom
   Encircle them 'round both by night and by day;
That many are mould'ring in ocean's drear
   tomb,
   And tears bring not back what your tide bore
   away.

Yet, sweet flowing River, my thoughts once again

Shall turn as in childhood all fondly to thee;
Deal kind with thy treasures — I'll love thee as
  when
My thoughts, like thy waters, danced out to
  the sea.

I DREAM.

———

I DREAM that all around is joy,
    That earth is pure as e'er it
      bloomed;
I dream of childhood, when a boy,
    In fancy airy castles loomed.

I dream of Fame's bewitching smile,
    A name to all the wide world dear;
I dream of things as free from guile
    As is a loving mother's tear.

I wake and find the world the same,
    I wake — the pleasures die away;

10

E'en he who wears the crown of fame
  Is hastening on to swift decay.

I wake and care soon casts its pall,
  The bustling world seems full of woe,
I see the young and aged fall,
  Friend after friend doth homeward go.

I see that all the loved on earth
  Must part though tears fall as the rain;
I mark grim sorrow joined to mirth,
  And health walk hand in hand with pain.

From childhood e'en to tottering age,
  We dream — we wake — and all is o'er !
The cares of life our minds engage —
  We live — we die — we dream no more !

THOUGHTS ON THE DEATH OF

MISS MARGARET DAVIDSON.

"And Death who called thee hence away,
Placed on his brow a gem of light."
MARGARET TO HER SISTER.

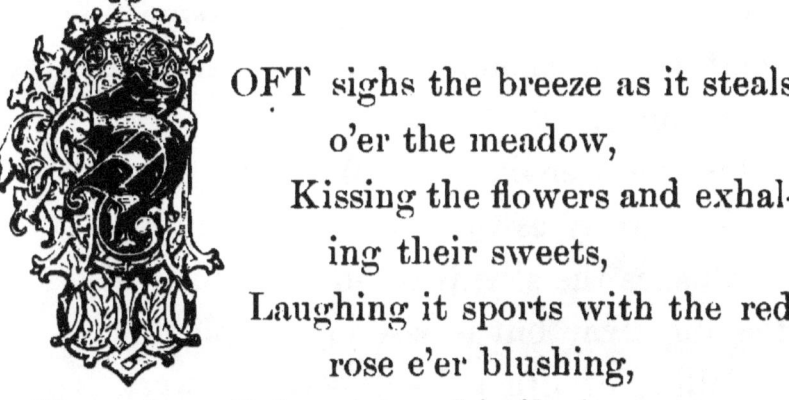

OFT sighs the breeze as it steals
o'er the meadow,
Kissing the flowers and exhal-
ing their sweets,
Laughing it sports with the red
rose e'er blushing,
Then the tall forest tree kindly it greets.
Now o'er the graves of the dear and departed,

Sighing it lingers as though it would stay;
Oh, it is sweet that though mortal must perish,
　Flowers spring above us and zephyrs will
　　play.
Margaret!—thy name on the marble I'm
　　reading,
　Sweet bird of song thou art sleeping full
　　well;
We upon earth beheld but thy dawning,
　Only angels above of thy present can tell.

Sadly I feel when I think that the fairest
　Flowers, in their beauty, must soonest decay;
Sombre's the thought when I hear that sweet
　　zephyr,
　Lisping, e'er lisping, "We're passing away!"
Passing away as the sun in the evening
　Blushes the sky as he sinks to his rest;
Passing away but to rise in his splendor,
　Telling of life as he dips in the west.

Soon to death's river thy pure spirit hastened,

Long on the banks thou entranced did'st
  stand;
Saw the bright glories — the splendor beyond
  thee —
Saw thy " Lucretia " in that golden land;
Saw all the loved who had passed o'er before
  thee,
  Heard the sweet music about the high throne;
'Twas but a step and the torrent was forded,
  Now with those rich notes thou minglest
  thine own.

TO A SNOW FLAKE.

INY little snow-flake falling
    from above,
Nestling on this dreary earth —
    kissing it with love,
Welcome little stranger,
    With thy numerous train,
Thou hast been a ranger,
    Welcome back again !

Tiny little stranger, tell me whence you come;
Tell me of the upper air — tell me of thy home !
    Tell me earth is calling
    For thy mantle white,
    Tell me thou art falling
    And her plains delight.

Dropping, dropping, dropping from the upper air
Tiny little stranger virtue's garb you wear;
     As God's grace is given,
     As his love descends,
    Softly falls from heaven
     With his children blends.
So from those far regions lovingly you fall,
Making earth look brighter—blessing nature all.
    Welcome little stranger
     With thy numerous train,
    Thou hast been a ranger,
     Welcome back again!

ODE OF WELCOME.

READ AT THE ORPHANS' HOME, BATH, NEW YEAR'S
EVE, JAN. 1, 1873.

 HAPPY Night, that doth appear
To crown the glory of the year!
Where Love keeps guard what
    need to roam?
And 'Love keeps guard around
    this home.

Our country's Wards! that dying prayer,
On southern fields, by angels care,
Was wafted to the Throne above,
And angel voices sang of love.

'Tis New Year's Eve and eyes grow bright,
And merry faces come to light;
Glad, happy hearts, you need not roam,
No cloud shall pass across your Home.

The song shall rise, the evening prayer
Shall give them to their Father's care;
Affection's flowers shall fresh appear,
And cluster 'round the dawning year.

What nobler sight to thrill the heart,
The loved and loving need not part;
Here safe at home no one need grieve,
For Pleasure guards the New Year's Eve.

Each star that shines in heaven above,
Shall twinkle down a Father's love;
Each eye that glistens here to-night,
Shall twinkle up a child's delight.

O happy Year, that brightly dawns,
Clear be thy nights and fair thy morns!
These childrens' voices ring out clear,
And wish you all a Glad New Year!
II

They thank you for your tender care,
They feel that you their pleasure share;
The rolling year must pass away,
Yet memory still can hold her sway.

This Home shall throw a fragrance round,
And where we stand 'tis holy ground;
The seed dropped tearful in the earth,
Shall blossom in triumphant birth.

They are our own! a country's pride!
Columbia keeps them by her side;
Beneath her care their feet may roam,
And Love still guards the Orphan's Home.

Then once again, with voices clear,
They wish you all a Glad New Year!
Their hearts are full and words are weak,
If thoughts were words how they would speak.

ONLY A CHILD.

ONLY a child that was killed in
    the street,
  Wandering there with her poor
    weary feet;
  "No one's to blame!" and the
    driver looked wild,
Saying, "It's lucky 'twas only a child!"

Only a child — yet the crowd presses on,
Take her away for the spirit has gone!
Gone from its anguish, its prison, its woe,
Up to its Maker who sent it below.

Pity her not, she had no loving home,
Father a drunkard — her fate was to roam;

Weary and hungry to beg for her bread,
Pity her not, for at last she is dead!

Hollow-eyed, ragged, deformed from her birth,
All have refused her a home but the earth;
Poor little feet that have wandered too long,
Pure, sinless heart that has ne'er known the
　　wrong.

Only a child — and there falleth no tear,
No one remains that will think of her here;
But 'mongst the blessed the Father sweet
　　smiled,
And angel-harps welcomed a glad, radiant
　　child.

COME TO ME.

OME to me when in sorrow I am
calling
    When darkness veils the sun and
        shows no day;
    When all I loved and prized are
'round me falling,
Come to me, darling — do not longer stay!

Come tell me stories that the past, so golden,
    Loved to repeat unto my listening ear;
Come tell me legends of the ages olden,
    I only wait to feel that thou art near.

Come to me song-bird on the joyous morrow,
   Thy notes shall soothe my heart and banish
      pain.
And from the sky shall pass the clouds of
      sorrow,
   If I but know that thou can'st come again.

Alas, alas, in vain my soul keeps crying,
   They may not come who cross death's rolling
      tide!
And only dirges to my voice replying,
   Chant thou art ever banished from my side.

A ROMANCE OF

NEW MEADOW'S RIVER.

FOUNDED ON FACT.

EW MEADOWS flows the same
    to-day,
    With dancing waters to the sea,
And tells her story all the way,
    Replete with love and melody.
The wild woods bend on either side,
    To cast their shadows in the stream,
And sunbeams sparkle on her tide,
    Like bright thoughts in a Poet's dream.

Fair River! few have sung thy praise,
   Unknown, thou murmurest to the sea,
But from the far-off, golden days,
   I hear these echoes come from thee.

Time was when on thy western shore
   The busy hum of trade did rise;
When Commerce in her hands upbore
   The products of far-distant skies.
The keel was stretched, the white-winged ship
   Launched on thy tide — then sped away,
And fleeing south her prow did dip
   Where Pleasure ruled the golden day.

Good, honest Burghers! time has fled,
   The crumbling mounds alone remain:
And those that lived and loved are dead,
   The mossy stones reveal no name.
In quiet church-yards they sleep well,
   Who planned and toiled in years gone by,
And thy sweet stream alone doth tell
   The tale of those who lived to die.

Haply some aged sire remains,
    Whose memory wanders almost back,
And reason for a moment reigns,
    To light the wanderer on his track.

Near "Howard's Point," the old bridge spanned,
    It, only, crossed New-Meadow's tide ;
And reached from smilling land to land,
    And long the elements defied.
A prosperous village nestled there,
    Ere Bath was known by even name,
The spire uprose, the pastor's prayer
    Breathed soft to heaven — 'tis e'er the same.

There "Nimmy " told the artless maid
    Her future fortune from the cup,
Who heard half-laughing, half-afraid,
    Then took the charmed goblet up ;
Or, at the dance, the rustic feet
    Tripped lightly to her wondrous song,
And all the village loved to greet
    And hear her charm the artless throng.

12

Poor "Nimmy!" youth since then has gone,
  And made their bed alike with thee;
The world's contempt and cruel scorn
  Have died away — for thou art free.

One summer day, by "Ragged Isle,"
  That frowns far out upon the sea,
When Nature wore her sunniest smile,
  And earth was full of melody,
A white-winged vessel sped along,
  Cape Small Point on the larboard bow,
And on her deck a motley throng,
  Where crime had branded every brow.
Bold rovers of the Spanish main,
  They turned from plunder on the deep;
Each hand imbued with Cain's red stain,
  Their victims 'neath the ocean sleep.

Onward they speed! New-Meadow's tide
  Now ripples round their vessel's prow;
Who walks alone, in sullen pride,
  A dark frown resting on his brow!

The captain of that restless band,
    Envenomed 'gainst the race of man ;
He gazes on the passing land,
    Then northward doth his vision scan.
" This is the place.   I know it well,"
    He mutters, " Ah, they chase in vain !
Nor winds nor waves can ever tell,
    Where floats the Rover of the Main !
Here in these northern wilds secure,
    The gold obtained by blood shall rest ;
My bark is fleet, my comrades sure,
    'Tis danger gives to life a zest !
Aye, fools are they who toil to win
    A· meagre pittance at the end,
Better to reap the spoils of sin,
    Who sins the most may most amend ! "

The bark speeds on ! the sun dips down
    Blood-red as blushing at the sight ;
The shadows fall — with sombre frown
    Advance the spectral forms of night.

Now " Howard's Point " comes into view,
  'Tis rounded on the western side;
And all elate the pirate crew
  Stand ready for what may betide.
The water shoals, but just ahead
  An island lifts its ghostly form,
Seeming as dropped in marshy bed,
  It rears its front 'gainst wind and storm.
To north and west the wood's dark shade
  Resounds with tones of insect life,
The struggling moon seems half afraid
  To look down on these men of strife.
O night that warps the world in sleep,
  And soothes earth's countless cares away,
How many secrets must you keep,
    If thou could'st speak what would'st thou
      say!
The mother's prayer thou bearest above,
  Beseeching for a wandering son,
And craving from the Throne of Love
  A blessing for the erring one.

Sweet time of night! how memory turns,
　And thoughts fly back and tumults cease;
The fire upon the altar burns,
　And night, in silence, whispers peace.

The sails are furled, the bark rounds to,
　The boat is lowered — they gain the strand,
Nor haunted by that murdered crew,
　They bring their treasures to the land,
Near where a grave-yard keeps its dead,
　Beneath a hill they dig the earth;
The stars alone look down o'erhead,
　Unmindful of the golden worth.

"There now, my boys," the Chief exclaims,
　"Our prize is safe, our land-marks sure,
In times to come when each one names
　His part, who then can count him poor?
Let's now away, for plunder calls,
　The merchantman sails on the sea,
Rich wealth within her oaken walls,
　It only sails for you and me."

They gained their craft — all sail was made,
  To scenes of rapine sped they on,
And when the morning lit the glade,
  All traces of that crew had gone.

* * * * * * * * * * * * *

The years sped by, time loiters not,
  Nor e'er turns back to view the past,
What was, perchance, is now forgot,
  What is, cannot forever last.
Full fifty years with magic sway,
  Had passed since sailed that pirate band,
And men had lived and passed away,
  And change was written o'er the land.
The old-worn bridge had passed from sight,
  The village now was hushed and still,
The day kept silence with the night,
  And "Nimmy" slept beneath the hill;
The river flowed unto the sea,
  As if no change had marked its path,
And telling of the yet to be,
  Pealed out the bells of distant Bath.

The engine yoked it to the car,
   And shrieked across New-Meadow's tide,
And cities sprung up near and far,
   Nor missed that from New-Meadow's side.

The sun was low — a wearied man
   Bowed down with years kept on his way,
And every object seemed to scan,
   And muttered, though he naught did say.
Where "Bull Bridge" spans New-Meadow's
     tide,
   He took his course — the day was cold, —
And one that passed near to his side
   Said that he muttered: "Gold, my gold!"
When o'er the bridge he turned him south,
   And craved a farmer's home to share,
"I'll pay you well!" came from his mouth.
   "I've gold and silver coins to spare."
He showed a chart — begrimmed with time —
   From "Howard's Point" to upper land,
At night he dug with murmuring rhyme:
   "The last one of the Pirate's band?"

He came, he went — he paid in gold;
  Old Spanish coin the farmer took;
His story ne'er by him was told, —
  The rustic trembled at his look.
Doubtless he only of that crew
  Had lived to reach his hidden wealth,
But gold stays not the year's adieu,
  Nor can give back departed health.
And even now the traveler stays,
  And marks where dug that ancient man,
The farmer to his closing days
  Will keep the pirate's time-worn plan.

TO A LAKE.

OUNTAINS around thee rise,
    Above, below, the skies!
The wild fawn, timid, from the
    leafy brake,
Starts at his imaged form, in
    thee, fair Lake!

The woods embrace thee 'round,
Each height with foliage crowned;
But few have e'er beheld thy virgin face,
Thou jewel set with Nature's loveliest grace.

The wild bird flies o'erhead,
Or, on thee, has no dread;

13

The little brook, that wooed thee through the
    day,
Melts with thy waters, into song, away.

Thou glassy Mirror, fair!
My thoughts are wandering where,
This summer day, thou laughest in thy pride,
And I, alas, am far from thy loved side!

For to earth's wearied mind,
A pleasure undefined
Thou bring'st to him who far from dusty street,
Communes with Nature in her own retreat.

Undine-like I see
Fair forms arise from thee;
And from thee come sweet words to cheer my
    heart —
I know thou chidest that I keep apart!

I shall be near thee soon;
The balmy breath of June

Shall greet me wandering 'neath thy wild-
 wood's shade,
Where oft o'er flowery banks my feet have
 strayed.

MISS DELLA POWERS,

DIED AT ORLAND, MAINE, OCTOBER, 1873.

Hor last words wero: "A little while my Father dear and I will meet you on tho other shore."

LITTLE while my Father dear,
And earthly anguish will be o'er,
Your darling Della only goes
To meet you on the other shore.
Bright angels touch their harps so
    sweet,
I now can hear their glad refrain,
Farewell, O loved ones, I depart
Yet I shall meet you all again.

The heavenly chorus swelled the song,
And earthly notes were borne above,
As Della joined the happy throng,
And touched her harp to sing of love.

" A little while my Father dear " —
How sweet those words to cheer the heart,
The loved on earth in heaven will meet,
Thank God there is no power to part!
The sun goes down at close of day,
To rise upon a brighter morn;
So your fair sun but dipped the west,
To shine the brighter when 'twas gone.

And though time pass with hast'ning feet,
That father e'er her voice can hear,
From o'er the tide with incense sweet,
That tells him that his child is near;
There is no grave in northern clime,
Nor ocean's depths although they roar,
Can keep the loved and lost on earth,
From meeting on the other shore.

THE IDEAL WORLD.

HERE is a land where the
sunbeams are glist'ning,
It is a land which all mortals
may know;
Often we rove there and stand
vaguely list'ning,
Reveling 'mid objects that dwell not below.

Bright are its plains with sweet flowers ever
blooming,

Time has no sway in that region sublime,
Castle and turret within it are looming,
What shall I say is the name of this clime?

It is the dream-land, of fancies the dwelling,
  It is the threshold of that great to be,
From whence the music of angel-harps swelling,
  Fills all our souls with its sweet melody.

Drear is this earth and its shadows are falling
  Over the pathway, perforce, we must tread;
Time never loiters — each second is calling
  Some one from life to the home of the dead;

But in our visions the loved, the departed,
  Come once again as in blest days of yore,
Drying the tears of earth's poor, broken-hearted,
  Telling of glories, of life evermore.

Is it ideal that the spirit, up-springing,
  Leaves its dull body to slumber below?
Death is but life! all the ages are ringing;
  Over the river we see the bright glow.

Hast thou not heard — 'tis a strange, ancient
    story,
  Of a fair island where death never came?

E'en the poor Indian has dreamed of its glory,
   And, dying, has whispered its sweet-breathing
     name!

Isle of the blessed! unseen o'er the ocean,
   Fancy has pictured thy regions sublime;
Life-giving streams in their musical motion,
   Wash out the foot-prints of death-dealing
     time.

Land of Immortals! your blue skies are smiling
   Somewhere, I know, though they're seen but
     in dreams;
Not as a mirage, deceptive, beguiling,
   Nor wholly departing at morning's bright
     beams.

Life is but thought! and should we call seeing
   With the dull eye, though the organ of sight,
All of our vision — the soul has a being
   Wandering at will through the regions of
     light.

Knowing no shackles, ne'er drooping, nor dying,
　Where the poor body must stop it can roam;
In the Ideal — and, methinks, it turns sighing,
　Joining with sorrow its poor, earthly home.

Nature is speaking — each bud in expanding,
　Cover the seed — 'tis the germ of the tree;
What is the lesson to our understanding?
　This is its teaching — Immortality!

Nothing is lost — though in gloom and in
　　sorrow
Death takes a loved one and bears him away,
The sun that goes down, sinks to rise on the
　　morrow,
　And light springs from darkness and life
　　from decay.

Is it ideal, when the soul, ever longing,
　Peoples a world with its visions of light?
Calling up objects that ever are thronging,
　Visions that come from the shadows of night?

14

Hast thou not gazed on the vast, surging ocean,
  Dashing its waves on the wild, craggy shore,
Telling and chanting, with deep-toned emotion,
  Tales of such grandeur ne'er thought of
    before;

Or in deep woods when the moonbeams are
    falling,
  When the dark shadows cause spectres to
    rise,
Hast thou not heard, as it were, a voice calling,
  As though the angels spoke soft from the
    skies?

Then to their maker, unconscious, we wander,
  Awe-stricken think — " And does he care for
    me?"
Is he not speaking, we ask, and we ponder,
  Dreaming sweet dreams of the life yet to be!

Call these but fancies—they yet have a meaning,
  Deeper than mortals, perchance, here can
    know;

He who in sorrow and gloom is now gleaning,
  May gather rejoicing — the harvest shall
  glow.

IN MEMORIAM.

J. L. BOOTHBY,

DIED AT BANGOR, APRIL 14, 1873.

 E giveth his beloved rest;
  What blessed words to cheer the
      heart !
  The hands now folded on the
      breast,
  No more must work life's bitter
      part.

He giveth his beloved rest;
  A tired child has gone to sleep,

A wave has died on ocean's breast,
  And sunk in silence on the deep.

The husband kind, the friend sincere,
  Has passed to the eternal shore;
Yet Love still guards his memory here,
  Although its treasure comes no more.

He giveth his beloved rest:
  What heavenly peace can He bestow!
Asleep upon the Savior's breast,
Oh, who would dwell fore'er below!

EPITAPH.

NOT that she loved earth less, but
    heaven more,
    And at a ripe old age, her
      work well done,
    Her Master called and in his
      arms upbore
A saintly Angel who the crown had won.

TWO CHILDREN.

WO children stood one Summer
    day
   Beneath the elm trees gently
    swaying,
   Whilst danced the happy hours
    away,
And life seemed only made for playing.
Their rippling laughter reached my ear,
   And, somehow, brought to me a sorrow,
For though the day was bright and clear,
   I thought upon a sad to-morrow.

Oh, happy children, laugh and play,
   What reck you of a sad to-morrow,

For though these hours must pass away,
   There comes to you no thought of sorrow.
Keep pure your hearts, and though time fade,
   And earthly ties and joys may sever,
There is a land that knows no shade,
   God's children dwell therein forever.

THE ARMY AND NAVY UNION.

FAIR Peace embraced a smiling
land,
And home our conquering
heroes came,
Then Mercy gave her sweet
command,
And blessings clustered 'round her name,
The *Union* answered to the call,
Whilst Love turned back no more to stray,
And heaven looked down and smiled on all, —
The night was long — how fair the day !

15

Blessed Union ! how thy name doth thrill,
   What memories come at thought of thee !
Thy stream flows soft, for every rill
   Springs from the fount of charity.
The banks are green on either side,
   Thy children seek the welcome shade,
And love and peace fore'er abide,
   For Mercy spoke and was obeyed.

•

SPRING.

TO our loved clime again a Maiden
    hies,
    At first too coy, with down-cast,
      modest eyes;
    The violets greet her and the
      song-birds sing
And trill the praises of their mistress, Spring!

Stern-winter's hand is loosed, the brook runs
    free,
The blade grows green, the bud adorns the tree,
Where'er her light step falls its trace remains,
And beauty nestles o'er our hills and plains.

Sweet time of Spring ! what memories flood the
heart

What dreams of rapture doth thy name impart !

She grows in beauty through the lengthening
hours,

And girlish Summer walks amongst her flowers.

SUMMER.

NOW rosy Summer from her throne
of flowers
Scatters sweet perfume through
the livelong day;
Babbling sweet words to charm
the happy hours,
She trips in pleasure and in song away.

The fields are green, or show their changing
hues,
The swallow's shadow swiftly skims the
ground,
Dame Nature's mirror gleams with countless
views,
And peace and plenty seem to smile around.

The brook pays tribute to the noon-day sun,
  And laughing children cross its shallow bed;
The woods resound with ring of huntsman's gun,
  The clouds seem sporting as they float o'er-
    head.

The night breathes still — if we can call that
    night,
  Which comes all radiant with its jeweled
    crown;
The moon rolls on — the stars with eyes of light
  Look from their ocean in contentment down.

Sweet time of Peace! the soul is upward drawn,
  We look to Him who made and giveth all;
Who made the light and gave the blessed morn,
  He knows each thought — He marks each
    sparrow's fall.

LOST.

GOOD ship sailed from a land-
    locked bay ·
Far out to the distant West,
And we watched her long as she
    sunk away,
    And thought of the time, of that
not far day,
She'd enter a port of rest!

She passed from sight and was seen no more;
Who knows how the billows tost,
How 'gainst the tempest and storm she bore
  And, perchance, went down near her destined
    shore

With the wild waves howling, " Lost ! "

'Tis a dismal sound — yet more sad each day
   Are the wrecks in this life we see;
For passion's waves have a fiercer sway
   For they whelm the soul with the mould'ring
     clay —
'Tis lost for eternity !

SAVED!

HE demon-wind shrieking,
    Its horrors bespeaking,
  We float but a hull on the wild,
    raging sea ;
  Do we speak — none can hear
    us,
The craggy shore near us,
And Death seems to mutter, "Just under the
  lee ! "

The lead gives its warning —
Each thought of the morning
Is pregnant with gloom, with a wreck on the
  shore,

14

But never despairing,
His face a smile wearing,
The sailor hopes on — he has left nothing more !

"Light ho !" is now ringing,
The beacon-light flinging
Its rays through the darkness shines clear to
  our sight,
And joy usurps sorrow,
We know that the morrow
Will find us safe anchored inside of the light.

Thus over life's surges,
When drear are its dirges,
And Hope almost leaves us cast down in deep
  fear,
The soul that ne'er chiding,
In God e'er confiding,
Is saved — for its refuge forever is near !

TO ETTA.

ALAS, the crimson autumn leaves
We gathered on that radiant day,
Have long since lost their brilliant
    hues —
And in their beauty passed away;

And Casco's island shines not bright,
As when we trod its lovely shore,
The wintry snows enshroud it now —
That golden Summer day is o'er.

Yet, Etta, though the seasons change,
Thou art to me fore'er the same,
And sunshine seems to gild the page,
On which I write my Etta's name!

FAREWELL!

AREWELL to you, Annie,
    October is sighing,
    And fate bids me wander
    o'er life's stormy sea;
    I ask the wild waves, but there
    comes no replying,
Will Annie, my Darling, e'er come back to me!

Farewell to you, Annie, in gloom and in sorrow
    I see my bright star sink in darkness away;
And I ask to myself if a bright sunny morrow
    Will dawn on the heart that has squandered
    its day!

Farewell to you, Annie, when Summer is smiling,
    And Casco's loved islands gleam fair in the sea,
Let me hope some bright hour, all my sorrow
    beguiling,
    That Fate will bring Annie, in beauty, to me!